Lions Aren't Scared of Shots

To my children, Molly and Ryan — HJB

To my two moms, Julie Weber and Minnie Herbst — MSW

Published by
MAGINATION PRESS
An Educational Publishing Foundation Book
American Psychological Association
750 First Street, NE
Washington, DC 20002

For more information about our books, including a complete catalog, please write to us,
call 1-800-374-2721, or visit our website at www.maginationpress.com.

Managing Editor: Darcie Johnston
Project Editor: Kristine Enderle
Art Director: Susan K. White
Printed by Worzalla, Stevens Point, Wisconsin

LIBRARY OF CONGRESS CATALOGING-IN-PUBLICATION DATA

Bennett, Howard J.
Lions aren't scared of shots : a story for children about visiting the doctor /
by Howard J. Bennett; illustrated by M.S. Weber.
   p. cm.
ISBN-13: 978-1-59147-473-9 (hardcover : alk. paper)
ISBN-10: 1-59147-473-6 (hardcover : alk. paper)
ISBN-13: 978-1-59147-474-6 (pbk. : alk. paper)
ISBN-10: 1-59147-474-4 (pbk. : alk. paper)
   1. Children — Medical examinations — Juvenile literature.
2. Sick children — Juvenile literature. 3. Physicians — Juvenile literature.
I. Weber, M. S. (Michael S.) II. Title.
RJ50.B46 2007
618.92—dc22   2006009579

10 9 8 7 6 5 4 3 2 1

Lions Aren't Scared of Shots

A Story for Children About Visiting the Doctor

by Howard J. Bennett, M.D.
illustrated by M.S. Weber

MAGINATION PRESS • WASHINGTON, D.C.

I went to see the doctor today.
My mom said it was time for my check-up.

When we got there, lots of kids were waiting to see the doctor.

"Do I have to get a shot?" I said. I hugged my dog Cinnamon.

"I'm not sure Molly-Bean.
Why don't you ask Dr. Ryan when we see him?" she said.

"I like seeing Dr. Ryan. But I don't like shots."

Nurse Carol took me to Dr. Ryan's
check-up room.

"Let's see how tall you are," she said.
I stood against the wall.

"Let's see how much you weigh,"
she said. I stood on a wiggly scale.

"Let's see how strong your heart
is pumping," she said.
Nurse Carol wrapped a band
around my arm
that made a tight squeeze.

"Hi, Molly," said Dr. Ryan when he came into the room.
"Wow, you've grown a lot taller.
Do you have any questions before we start your check-up?"

"Do I need a shot?" I said.

"That's a good question.
I'm going to check your body first, and then
I'll give you an answer. Does that sound fair?"

"Wait a second," Dr. Ryan said.
"I didn't know you were a monkey."

"I'm not a monkey," I said.

Dr. Ryan checked my arms and shoulders.
"Your arms are very strong," he said.
"I bet you could swing from the highest branches in the jungle."

Dr. Ryan pushed on my tummy and tickled my belly button.
"I see you don't have fur on your body. Monkeys have lots of fur,
so I guess you're not a monkey."

Dr. Ryan put on his stethoscope and said,
"I didn't know you were an elephant. Is that a trunk?"

"I'm not an elephant," I said.

Dr. Ryan listened to my heart and lungs.
"Your heart and lungs sound great," he said.
"I bet you could jump rope all day."

Dr. Ryan looked at my hands.

"Your skin is smooth.

Elephants have rough skin, so I guess you're not an elephant."

Dr. Ryan said, "I didn't know you were a kangaroo.
Look at the size of those feet."

"I'm not a kangaroo," I said.

Dr. Ryan tapped my knees and ankles with a little hammer.
"Your legs look pretty strong to me," he said.
"I bet you could jump higher than the moon."

Dr. Ryan turned on his light and looked in my mouth and ears.
"Your ears are kind of small.
Kangaroos have big ears, so I guess you're not a kangaroo."

Dr. Ryan asked me to read some letters on the wall and said,
 "I didn't know you were an eagle. Are those wings?"

"I'm not an eagle," I said.

Dr. Ryan shined a light in my eyes and asked me to look up and down.
 "Your eyes are perfect," he said.
 "I bet you could find a mouse playing hide and seek."

Dr. Ryan looked in my nose and gave it a little squeeze.
"Your nose is soft.
Eagles have hard beaks, so I guess you're not an eagle."

Dr. Ryan asked me to stand up and said,
"I didn't know you were a giraffe.
When did you get such a long neck?"

"I'm not a giraffe," I said.

Dr. Ryan asked me to touch my toes and stand up straight.
"You're pretty tall," he said.
"I bet you could see over everyone's head at the movies."

Dr. Ryan looked at my neck and back.

"You don't have any spots.

Giraffes have lots of spots, so I guess you're not a giraffe."

Dr. Ryan said,
"Let's see. You have strong arms and legs,
a great heart, terrific eyes and ears,
a straight back, smooth skin,
a nice pink nose, ten fingers and toes,
two hands, and you are very tall.
Why you must be…

a healthy, five-year-old!"

"Does that mean I don't need a shot?" I said.

Dr. Ryan patted Cinnamon.

"Actually, Molly, you need one shot.
It will help keep you healthy and strong.
It will feel like a quick sting,
and if you imagine you're a monkey swinging in the jungle
or an eagle soaring overhead, you won't notice it so much."

Nurse Carol came back to the room and said,
"Molly, are you ready?"

"I'm not Molly!" I roared.
"I'm a lion, and lions aren't scared of shots!"

Note to Parents

by Jane Annunziata, Psy.D.

The doctor is friendly. The nurses are cheerful. The office is warm and colorful, with picture books and a video playing in the waiting room. Nevertheless, children can still feel uneasy about their medical visits. When parents understand what causes this anxiety and how to help their child cope, these appointments can be significantly less stressful—for children and parents both!

Children worry about visiting the doctor for many reasons. Perhaps most obvious, these visits are often associated with physical discomfort (e.g., a sore throat, a broken bone, a high fever), and they can lead to unpleasant outcomes, such as a bad-tasting medicine or a nebulizer treatment. The visit itself may involve procedures that hurt, such as a shot; or activities that seem strange, such as a blood pressure cuff tightening around the arm; or procedures that feel very intrusive, such as a throat culture.

Medical visits place children in a vulnerable position. They feel physically vulnerable because they may be feeling unwell, and because they may be undressed, in which case they likely feel cold and embarrassed. Older children can also feel psychologically vulnerable, because they are more likely to worry that something is wrong with their bodies.

Finally, children feel an inherent loss of control when taken to the doctor, which can spark anxiety and sometimes anger too. They have to do something they don't want to do, they don't have a choice about it, and they have to submit to whatever the doctor says. This is especially awful when the recommendation is something as dreaded as a shot!

Easing Your Child's Anxiety

Of the many things parents can do to minimize their child's anxiety, the first is the most simple: Embrace the belief that visits to the doctor don't have to be unduly stressful. Parents sometimes communicate to their children (often indirectly) that the visit is destined to end in tears and meltdowns. This does not have to be the norm. Adopt as your goal and mindset that you will do everything you can to have these visits go well. Communicate this directly to your children, as well as indirectly through your attitude and demeanor.

Other practical, proactive things parents can do before, during, and after doctor visits include the following:

- Make sure the doctor (along with his or her practice) is a good fit for you and your child. Most physicians offer parents a "get to know the doctor" interview. Some parents like to bring their children with them to this appointment to see how they respond and to see how the doctor and staff interact with their child. If you are comfortable, your child will likely respond well too. Also, keep in mind that you will be working with the doctor's staff; it is important that you feel comfortable with them as well.

- Communicate to your child how much you like the doctor and the medical practice, using age-appropriate words. You might say, "I met a new doctor today that I really liked. She is very nice and really likes kids. She has a fun waiting room, with lots of neat toys." Your child will follow your positive lead and absorb your good feeling.

- If possible, schedule your child's first appointment as a wellness check (that does not require shots) or a quick introduction to meet the doctor. It is most helpful if the child's initial meeting is a positive one, not associated with illness or uncomfortable procedures.

- Give children advance notice about wellness appointments. This helps with feelings of loss of control. Also, let children know why they are going to the doctor (flu shot, check-up, sick visit, etc.). Emphasize that check-ups help them to stay healthy and feel good, and sick visits treat a medical problem so that they can feel better. It is easier for children to endure an unpleasant medical intervention if they understand why they have to have it. Thus, it helps to say to your child, "I know you hate these nebulizer treatments, but you've been having a lot of trouble with your breathing lately, and this will make breathing much more comfortable."

- Always be honest about the purpose of the visit. Parents sometimes want to avoid giving children information that will upset them (such as having to get a shot). However, avoidance on the front end inevitably causes worse reactions later and can create unnecessary negative reactions in the future.
- Remain calm and composed during exams and interventions. This soothes children and reassures them that nothing terrible is going to happen. Youngsters absorb the attitudes of their parents, and they role model a calm, matter-of-fact attitude if that is what they see.

Coping During the Doctor Visit

Despite all your efforts, children will sometimes feel uncomfortable or anxious during a visit with the doctor. No one knows better than you what works to calm and soothe your youngster; don't hesitate to use techniques you have found helpful in other contexts. In addition to your tried-and-true methods, these suggestions may help:

- Make sure your child understands what the doctor or nurse will be doing before it occurs. If the practitioner doesn't explain (e.g., "Now I'm going to shine a bright light in your eyes"), provide a simple explanation yourself (e.g., "It looks like the nurse is about to take your temperature"). This is especially important if an uncomfortable intervention is coming.
- Demonstrate medical procedures on yourself first if your child is resistant or apprehensive. For example, if your child does not like the tightness of the blood pressure cuff, let the doc-

tor take your blood pressure first. Calmly explain how the procedure feels. This not only role models calmness, but clearly shows the child that there is nothing uncomfortable about the medical intervention.

- Give your child some say over medical procedures whenever possible. For example, if the doctor or nurse doesn't do it automatically, you might ask if your child can pick which finger gets pricked when blood needs to be taken, which arm gets chosen for a shot, or even which band aid gets put on a cut. Children feel better when they have even a little bit of control.
- Use simple relaxation techniques when children start to get anxious. Helping them to practice deep breathing or visualize something pleasant or empowering can reduce anxiety. Also, talking children through the anxiety can be calming (e.g., "I know you don't like it when the doctor puts that instrument in your ear, but it doesn't hurt, and he's just checking to see what your ear looks like inside"). Finally, remind them of any relaxation techniques they have used successfully in the past.
- Reassure your child that any discomfort will be short lived, and use concrete ways to communicate this. You might say, "I'm going to count to five, and by then the shot will be over" or "In just a little while we'll be all finished and on our way home." Remind your child of how good he or she will feel when the procedure is over. It is also helpful to give something concrete to look forward to. Even something simple like stopping at the park on the way home or a reminder of a favorite TV show that night helps children through the rough moments. This is also a good time to reinforce children's bravery and remind them of the good feeling that comes when we master our anxieties and get through hard things.
- Bibliotherapy can be a helpful tool. This book, for example, is psychologically helpful because it shows a child finding a brave way to cope with a fear, which inspires other children to do the

same thing. It also normalizes fears associated with medical interventions and helps children realize they are not alone. And it shows a technique for mastering anxiety that children can use to feel brave and capable when confronted with an anxiety-provoking situation.

When parents understand children's medical concerns and help them manage their anxiety about a visit to the doctor, they teach their children not only how to cope with one worry, but also—and more broadly—the life lesson that anxiety can be overcome. Children discover a great feeling of mastery that occurs when they push through difficult situations and come out the other side— an experience they will transfer to many other life situations.

Jane Annunziata, Psy.D., is a clinical psychologist with a private practice for children and families in McLean, Virginia. She is also the author of many books and articles addressing the concerns of children and their parents.

About the Author

HOWARD J. BENNETT, M.D., practices pediatrics in Washington, D.C., and lives in Maryland with his wife and two children.
He is the author of a self-help book written for children and parents titled *Waking Up Dry: A Guide to Help Children Overcome Bedwetting.*
Dr. Bennett is also a clinical professor of pediatrics at the George Washington University School of Medicine and a member of the Community Advisory Staff at the Children's National Medical Center.
He maintains a web site (www.wakingupdry.com) where he posts bedwetting related information.

About the Illustrator

M.S. (MICHAEL) WEBER is a graduate of the Art Institute of Chicago. His illustrations have been featured in several children's magazines and online at Magickeys.com. "I look upon children as a new frontier," he says, "because if children are well influenced through their parents, education, and literature, the chances of our world becoming a better place will improve. This is why I illustrate children's stories." He lives in Chicago with his wife, stepdaughter, and lots of love sponges (aka cats).